Paying for the Past

Racy Reunions Book 1

By Sylvia McDaniel

Books by Sylvia McDaniel

Contemporary Romance

Standalones
The Reluctant Santa
My Sister's Boyfriend
The Wanted Bride
The Relationship Coach
Her Christmas Lie
Secrets, Lies, and Online Dating
Paying for the Past
Cupid's Revenge

Anthologies
Kisses, Laughter & Love
Christmas with you

Collaborative Series

Magic, New Mexico
Touch of Decadence

Western Historicals

Standalones
A Hero's Heart
A Scarlet Bride
Second Chance Cowboy

The Cuvier Women
Wronged
Betrayed
Beguiled

Lipstick and Lead
Desperate
Deadly
Dangerous
Daring
Determined
Deceived

Scandalous Suffragettes
Abigail
Bella
Callie
Faith

The Burnett Brides
The Rancher Takes a Bride
The Outlaw Takes a Bride
The Marshal Takes a Bride
The Christmas Bride

Anthologies
Wild Western Women
Courting the West
Wild Western Women Ride Again

Collaborative Series

The Surprise Brides
Ethan

American Mail Order Brides
Katie

Paying for the Past
Published by Virtual Bookseller

Cover Design by Kim Killion
thekilliongroupinc.com/

Formatting by Laurelle Procter
laurelleprocter@gmail.com

Copyright © 2015 by Sylvia McDaniel
This book and parts thereof may not be reproduced in any form, stored in a retrieval system, or transmitted in any form by any means—electronic, mechanical, photocopying, or otherwise—without prior written permission of the author and publisher, except as provided by the United States of America copyright law. The only exception is by a reviewer who may quote short excerpts in a review.

Short Description: Teacher Olivia Spencer sacrificed the man she loved for his career. Now she moonlights as an escort and they meet again.

ISBN: 978-1-942608-25-7 (paperback)
ISBN: 978-1-942608-26-4 (e-book)

{Contemporary Romance – Fiction}
{Romantic Comedy – Fiction}
{Romance – Fiction}

www.SylviaMcDaniel.com

Synopsis

Dr. Anthony DeAngelo holds patients' hearts in his hands, but is unwilling to take time from his career to find love for himself. Since the day his fiancé left him at the altar, his career has been his focus. Now that he's accomplished his career goals and become the nation's top cardiac surgeon, he finds it lonely at the top. Secretly he longs for a wife and family. Someone to love him.

Teacher Olivia Spencer is forced to moonlight as an escort to help put her siblings through college. She's dedicated her life to raising her orphaned brother and sister and sacrificed the man she loved for his career until the night he steps into her limo.

In this sexy, short contemporary romance can this couple overcome their past and find love in each other's arms once again?

Table of Contents

Chapter One 1

Chapter Two 16

Chapter Three 21

Chapter Four 31

Chapter Five 38

Chapter Six 51

Chapter One

Dr. Anthony DeAngelo hurried across the elegant hotel room to answer the telephone's annoying ring. He picked up the receiver and glanced out at the Dallas sky line. Being home brought back memories he'd rather forget. Memories that even after ten years left a hole in the pit of his stomach and his mind wondering what if. Memories of a tall blonde woman with voluptuous curves and a sweet laugh that he'd never forgotten.

"Yes," he said curtly.

"Your car is here," the bell captain informed him.

"Thank you," he said, and disconnected the call. For the hundredth time he redid his tuxedo tie. His hands were worth millions and could tie off a vicryl suture in his sleep, but he couldn't secure a satin bow tie. If he had a woman to help him, that would be great, but being the most sought after cardiac surgeon in the United States had drawbacks.

No personal life.

When you spent twelve to fifteen hours a day in the hospital, six and seven days a week, any relationship you might try to create ended up on life support. He'd pulled the plug more times than he cared to remember.

Tonight, on one of the biggest events of his life, he'd had to resort to having his assistant find him a paid escort. At thirty-five, in the top of his profession and yet he'd had to compensate a woman to appear on his arm so he wouldn't look like a pathetic loser. One without a significant other who spent more time in a sterile environment wearing gloves, not touching skin against skin, and not feeling a woman's arms wrapped around him each night.

This was worse than being rejected by every girl he'd asked to senior prom. Sure he'd been a nerd, but you would have thought some teenage girl would have wanted to go to the prom with the valedictorian.

And now history repeated itself. He'd flown in from New York to his hometown of Dallas and there had been no one to accompany him. Refusing to appear in front of his colleagues without a date, he'd paid this woman to share the night to celebrate his biggest accomplishment.

For the money she charged, you'd think beauty and sex were guaranteed. But no, the contract he'd signed specifically said he understood there would be no doing the nasty tonight. She was his paid date for the evening and the limo would take her home. Just like Cinderella, her magical coach disappeared at the stroke of midnight with or without him.

He grabbed his wallet and stuffed it in his tuxedo pants along with his key card and hurried out the door. Walking the short distance to the elevator, he wondered what he would tell everyone when this beautiful woman appeared by his side tonight.

Raylene, his assistant, had sent him an email and explained to him in rather candid detail that the agency said do not hire her if you expected sex and he'd laughed at her wording. He'd left the details up to Raylene, but told her he expected elegance, refinement and class.

Not a Harry Hines hooker.

As he stepped off the elevator, he walked through the prestigious hotel and was glad that he'd waited too long to get a room where the event was being held. This way he was away from the watchful eyes of his colleagues. This way no one would know that he traveled alone.

The bellman opened the door. "Dr. DeAngelo your limo is in the drive."

"Thank you," he said, and walked into the cool air.

Another bellman opened the limo door giving him a glimpse of a long shapely leg peeking from a side split. Her sparkling do-me high heels with straps around dainty feet sent his blood flowing into overdrive.

That rush of adrenaline at the sight of a woman's body felt good, damn good, considering that normally the only time he experienced that natural drug was when he was trying to save someone's life. When his hands were inside a patient's chest as he massaged their new heart and the elation of feeling it beat once again.

God, this was going to be a fun night with this delicious eye-candy on his arm as he celebrated his success. Too bad it wasn't…oh no, just because he was back in town did not mean that he'd think of her. Erase that thought before it went any further.

"Have a good night, sir," the bellman said.

Anthony slid into the limo and turned to say hello. His mouth twisted, his heart slammed in his chest at a rate that he knew wasn't good.

"Is this some kind of joke?" he spat. There sat none other than Olivia Spencer, his old girlfriend, his ex-fiancé. The name he'd erased from his thoughts just seconds ago.

$\sim$

Olivia knew her mouth was wide open, but she couldn't help but stare. Pain gripped her chest, tightened her lungs and left her reeling. Even after all these years the sight of Tony DeAngelo left her staggering.

Of all the dates, since she'd become an escort in the last year, she hadn't expected to see her old flame, her ex-fiancé, the man she'd left standing at the altar. "God no, I didn't know it was you."

He shook his head. "You gave up marrying me, to become a damn hooker."

Olivia leaned forward and hit the button on the window between her and the driver. "Stop. I'm getting out."

Sure there were bills to pay, but nothing said she had to stay. Any time she felt in danger the agency had given her the right to leave. Her head and her heart were in serious jeopardy - and she wasn't talking about the game show.

"What the hell are you doing?" he said.

"I'm not a hooker and I can leave any time I feel threatened. I'm getting out."

The driver pulled over and stopped.

"Isn't this our history?" he said. "You get scared and run."

"And you're still just as much of a jerk as you've always been. I'm not a damned hooker."

His laugh sounded ugly in the dark. Then he sighed and the noise was just poignant enough to make her stop and take notice. It was one of those, 'God, I don't want to do this, but I have no choice' groans.

"I need an escort tonight."

"I'll see if the agency can send someone else. Maybe it's not too late."

Spending the evening with Doctor Pain-In-The-Ass, was not exactly what she'd had planned.

"Hardly, the event starts in twenty minutes. There's no time. I'll be on my best behavior if you'll just stay."

She raised her brows. The money from tonight alone would be enough to buy Caitlyn's books for the next semester. But still there was a wedding fiasco, two broken hearts, a linebacker mother and a conniving father between them. No need to resurrect the pain that had taken her years to overcome. Yet there were bills for Caitlyn's tuition. "Two conditions. We don't talk about the past and you're civil to me."

He looked down his nose at her, reminding her so much of his greedy mother who'd feared that she was jeopardizing her son's brilliant career.

"I accept your two and raise you one," he said. "You're to smile and be a consummate actress tonight. Play like you're my girlfriend. Like we're lovers and you're hanging on my every word. You use to be excellent at deception."

The jerk! She'd loved him heart and soul with every fiber of her being. She'd been young, in love, and totally smitten with boy wonder.

"Shut up, Tony, or I'm walking."

Pretending would be easy considering the memories of what a great lover he'd been flooded her senses when he'd stepped into the limo. They'd been young, in love and so good together. She'd dreamed they would spend their life with one another up until the accident and his family's reaction.

"Well, now you know what I want."

"At least you're clear today about what you want, not like when we were younger."

He stared at her. "I thought we weren't going to talk about the past."

"Agreed."

"But you had to get that last shot in, didn't you?"

She nodded, a feeling of satisfaction draped her conscience. Why had he never married? Whenever she thought about him, she'd always imagined him with a rich socialite of his mother's choosing on his arm, his practice going well with two or three spoilt children playing in the background.

Not a loner that had no one.

"Driver, go ahead," she told him and pushed the button on the window, closing the portal between them. She could do this for one night.

They sat in the car, silence hung smothering them like a wet blanket. "Normally, I ask my clients to tell me about their event. With you, I imagine it's something medical."

"It's the Reconstructive Heart Surgery Foundations annual event," he said quietly. "My colleagues from around the world are here tonight. I'm giving the keynote speech."

She nodded, very impressed. So he'd achieved his goals and made his bitch mother and money-worshipping father happy. But he'd never married.

"That's why I needed someone here tonight. I didn't want to go alone. Plus, I don't live here any longer, so I don't have the connections I once had," he explained, clearly uncomfortable that he'd had to resort to an escort service.

"So what do you want me to do?" she asked.

"Smile, shake hands and speak when spoken to. Don't try to build your client list tonight. Don't advertise that you're from an escort service. In fact, anything that is said is strictly confidential. Do you understand what I'm saying?"

"Yes, sir. Should I tell people my real name or make one up?" she asked, making her lips all pouty. "After all you think I'm a hooker."

"A damn high priced one, if you are," he said. "Just act natural, but keep your mouth shut."

"Whatever you want," she replied and leaned back against the seat. After all, he was the client, even though he'd once been her lover, her soul mate or so she believed. Tonight she'd give him what he wanted, take his money and then run like hell.

Ten years had passed since she'd left him at the altar. His eyes were still that same brilliant blue that melted her insides when he stared, but now there were crow's feet at the edges and a splattering of gray in his hair.

Yet his body still looked firm beneath his tux. Firm enough that her nipples had perked to attention like a soldier at full salute. Sex between the two of them had been hotter and wetter than a steam sauna. No man had ever wrung her out and left her fantasizing about their next sexual encounter. Tony's fingers could do the walking, the talking and have you moaning in a matter of seconds. He'd been damn good in bed.

He glanced at her, those blue eyes reaching inside and flipping on all her switches. Her sexual motor had been reawakened and idled at a slow hum. Just what she didn't need.

"You wouldn't happen to know how to tie a bow tie would you?"

She smiled and wondered if what the school newsletter said about him was true. He was in the last year of his residency when they'd become engaged. Quickly, she pushed the thoughts of the two of them from her mind. That year had been a tragic time in her life, one that changed things forever.

"I wondered if you always wore your tuxedo ties sideways or if you were starting a new fashion trend," she said giving him her best condescending gaze.

"I'm a world famous cardiology surgeon whose hands are worth millions and I can't tie a simple tuxedo tie," he said, clearly frustrated at his lack of skill.

She smiled feeling the tension inside the car ease slightly. "Let me. That's what I'm here for tonight."

Leaning into him, she pressed her body against his arm as he turned towards her and she untied his attempt. Quickly, she flipped the loops and doubled it over and then dropped the other side down and pulled the second end through the bow she'd created. Gently she straightened the tie just as the limo hit a pothole, sending her crashing into him.

A flurry of tingles like a snowstorm in July rushed through her at the feel of his chest against hers. He wrapped his hands around her arms and gently set her back on her side of the car. Heat radiated from his gaze.

Suddenly, she knew he'd felt those same tingles that had buzzed through her veins. He wasn't immune.

Her breath, caught in her throat. The center of her body hummed with a need she'd forgotten. Oh God, all these years later and this man still had the ability to make her body sing. And not a simple melody, oh no, he would have her singing the Hallelujah Chorus in three part harmony.

"Your tie looks much better now."

The grimace on his face almost looked painful. "Thanks."

Olivia sat back, smoothed her dress and gazed out at the downtown skyline as the limo zipped through town. After that little encounter, maybe she should go home. Obviously, her anatomy still had memories of the two of them. When she'd slammed into his chest, she'd felt like she'd come home. Home to the man she'd once loved and worshipped, until she'd set him free to become the man he was today.

He became all business. "We'll be sitting with the President of the Medical School and his wife. There may be some of the board of directors at the table as well as the director of the hospital where I currently work."

"Okay, I'll do my best not to embarrass you."

He glanced over at her and frowned. "You were never an embarrassment."

"Not even when my parents were killed driving drunk?"

"I thought we weren't going to talk about the past."

"Sorry, you're right, we weren't."

Silence filled the car as it whisked them toward the party Olivia was even more nervous attending than before. She took a deep breath, she could do this. She could smile and act cordial while putting on a haughty air that most of the time kept people from asking questions. Questions she could never answer.

"How are Caitlyn and Jason?"

Olivia sighed and took a deep calming breath. "Jason is in the military. He's at West Point and Caitlyn is a senior in college."

"Sounds like they're doing okay."

What he didn't know were the struggles the three of them had endured over the years. Struggles of raising two children on a teacher's salary with a pittance of an insurance settlement to secure their future.

"Why did you become an escort?" he asked staring at her like he couldn't believe what he was seeing. "You have a degree. You're a teacher, for God's sake. Why would you degrade yourself so?"

She laughed. "Like you would understand. Do you know how much teachers make? You probably make in one surgery what I make all year."

Other than the fact that college costs had stripped what was left of the insurance policy and sent her searching for a second job. One where she wasn't pimping cologne or working every night.

"Being someone's eye candy is better than phone sex and the pay helps cover the costs of books and tuition."

"What happened to the insurance money?" he asked.

"College isn't cheap. Jason sacrificed by getting a full scholarship to the naval academy, and promising to serve his country for the next ten years. Being an escort is the least that I can do."

She'd do whatever it took to help her brother and sister. They deserved better than what life had given them when they were so young.

It wasn't their fault that their parents were drunks who'd robbed them of their childhood and forced their sister to become their guardian.

The limo pulled up to the hotel and a doorman opened the car door, ceasing any further talk of her reasons for becoming a paid escort.

Tony stepped out of the limo and offered her his hand, helping her out of the car. She looked up into his big blue eyes and a shiver of nerves scurried down her spine. Placing her hand in his, she met his gaze and a sizzle flared in her midsection. One that had her breath shuddering.

The boy she'd known and loved in college had become a handsome man she found hard to believe was unattached.

The skirt of her dress flowed around her and slid up her thighs as she stepped from the car. Hurriedly, she covered herself. When she stood, she placed her hand in the crook of his arm.

"Here we go," he said and she realized he was nervous. Seldom had she ever seen him a bundle of nerves. Only when he'd been waiting to hear where he'd be doing his residency…then he'd been overwrought and more agitated than a cat in heat.

This confident doctor who held people's hearts in his hands and put them back together was trembling slightly.

"You're the best cardiac surgeon in the country, you'll do fine."

"So you've checked me out online." He didn't look at her as they walked into the hotel.

"The alumni association is always touting your name," she said. "And I've looked you up once."

He turned and gazed at her. "Too bad you had to look me up. You could have shared my last name and had a front row seat to my life."

She smiled sweetly at him. "No talking about the past. We're focused on tonight."

$\sim$

Tony walked into the hotel and towards the reception area. "Remember you're to smile and look beautiful tonight."

"I know. I'm here as decoration."

"Yes," he said as they walked up to the receiving table.

"Dr. DeAngelo," a woman said, running towards him. "We're so glad to see you. I was beginning to fear you'd been held up in New York."

He smiled. "Barbara, I would have contacted you to let you know if my flight were delayed."

"I know, but I couldn't help but worry." She glanced over at Olivia. "And just who is this, beautiful woman Dr. DeAngelo? I didn't know you were married."

For a moment, he was tempted to let the woman assume that Olivia was his wife, but that had come so close to the truth that maybe it would be better to halt those rumors before they were started. "This is Olivia Spencer, a friend."

"Nice to meet you," Barbara said, in her very southern drawl. "I can't remember a time I've seen Dr. DeAngelo with a woman."

Why couldn't women keep their mouths shut? Like he wanted that fact advertised.

Olivia laid her other hand on his arm and gazed up at him adoring. "I know for a fact he's quite the ladies' man."

That was a sarcastic exaggeration that even he recognized. Women gravitated towards him, but they never stayed for long.

The last time he'd heard that Texas twang that was so much a part of home was when his mother and father visited him in New York.

"Work keeps me very busy," he said. "You women are a demanding lot. I've found it's better to involve myself in my first love, cardiology."

"Now you know more single men die of a heart attack than those who are married," Barbara admonished.

"Yes, but that's because they eat the worst food in the world. Me, I'm careful about what I eat and I make it to the gym regularly."

Olivia stood beside him, smiling, looking beautiful and silent while he talked drivel with this silly woman who ran tonight's event. His secretary had dealt with her most of the time. Thank God she'd kept her away from him. Damned if he wouldn't give Raylene a raise when he returned to work.

"We better find our seats," Tony said trying to walk away.

"Yes, you're at the reserved table up at the front. Several other guests are already seated."

"Thanks, Barbara," he said and turned back towards Olivia.

"That was painful." He gazed down at her. She smelled like sweet rain and sunshine and the memory of the two of them playing at the beach rocked him to his core. The image of her in that cute little turquoise two-piece had his mind rolling the tape of how he'd gotten her in the water, deep enough to slide that bottom clean off. They'd rode more than one wave that day, cresting at the same time.

"I know I'm not supposed to say anything, but you're zoning out," she said, tugging on his sleeve.

"Let's find our seats. The banquet is about to start."

Pulling her through the crowd, several people stopped and said hello before they finally reached their table. After he introduced her to everyone, he held out her chair.

The years had been good to her. She'd matured, her grace and elegance was beautiful and he would have been proud to have called her his wife. But that didn't happen. Instead, he'd gone to New York to finish his residency and she'd stayed here to go to work for the school district.

"Dr. DeAngelo," she said, squeezing his arm.

"Sorry, I was trying to remember if I brought my speech. I'm sure I did," he said, absently. How had he ever let her go? Why had she left him standing on the altar alone while his mother offered consoling words of comfort.

A frown wrinkled her brow. "You were always notoriously bad at remembering anything that didn't have to do with medicine. Check your pockets."

He patted his tuxedo, searching inside his jacket. "Crap, I think I left it on the counter. I was fiddling with my tie when the limo driver called. I bet it's still lying on the table by the door."

She shook her head at him. "Give me your assistant's name. What is her telephone number?"

"We've got to go back to the hotel," he said, frantically getting ready to stand and make a mad dash out the door. "I think I have time to get back to the hotel and pick it up."

She squeezed his arm tighter. "No, what is your assistant's phone number?"

"Raylene is on speed dial. I don't know her number. It's in my contacts."

Why the hell was she wasting his time? He needed to get back to the hotel and pick up his speech and he had to get going now.

"Give me your phone," she demanded.

He handed it over, not caring what she did with the contraption. She stood from the table and walked far enough away that no one could hear her. He watched her talking animatedly and then she looked in his direction and winked at him. The woman was incorrigible. This wasn't funny.

She'd already made an ass of him once in his life, was she going to do it a second time? Was she going to let him get in front of his colleagues, the biggest names in medicine and babble like a rambling psych professor without linear thinking?

Olivia walked back to the table, squeezed his shoulder, leaned over and said, "I'll be right back."

Of all the stupid stunts he'd pulled. He'd give Olivia just a little more time and then he was taking a cab to the hotel. He'd be back in thirty minutes. Patients had waited longer than that to see him and surely this group of doctors knew that sometimes schedules had to change to reflect their needs.

"Excuse me," he said, rising from the table. He had to find a cab and get to his notes. He'd tell Barbara before he walked out the hotel and even give the taxi driver a large tip to get him back as soon as possible.

He reached the door of the banquet room and saw Olivia meandering towards him and his penis hardened at the sight. God, she looked stunning in her black dress that fitted her trim body, the skirt opening to reveal a glimpse of her long legs in heels that screamed fuck me.

In her hand, she held something, a smile graced her full lips, her eyes twinkling in that way that had attracted him the first time they met. She walked up to him and handed him the papers.

"Here you go," she said her emerald eyes teasing. "You didn't think I could do it, did you?"

He glanced at the papers she'd shoved into his hand. His speech. "How did you get this?"

She smiled, took his hand and started to lead him back into the banquet room. "Your assistant emailed them to your phone. She has remote access into your office files and when she sent them, I went to the office center and printed them off."

"I'd have been frantic trying to get back to the hotel and here."

"Yes," she said, smiling at the people who parted for them while staring at the gorgeous piece of eye candy on his arm. His colleagues had never seen him with a woman before. A beautiful, intelligent woman that somehow he'd let get away.

What had changed that morning of the wedding? What had made her abandon the dreams of the two of them together? They'd been happy, or so he believed.

He stared at her, realizing how she'd just saved him from making a complete ass of himself in front of everyone or being overwhelmed as he urgently went back to his hotel room to find his missing speech.

"Thank you," he said.

"Any time," she replied as he pulled out her chair and she slide back into her role as his girlfriend, which was a role she'd chosen to step out of so long ago.

God, he wanted to remain angry at her for walking away from him. Yet somehow she was making him look great. The woman was smart, beautiful, and the two of them had been poised to set the world on fire. So why had she left him standing on the altar waiting for her to walk down that aisle and commit to being his wife? Why had she shamed him in front of his family and friends and confirmed his mother's suspicions?

He sank into a chair beside her and stuffed the speech into his inside pocket. She owed him some answers and sometime tonight, he would learn the truth before letting her go permanently.

An older woman, Mrs. James Thorton III, his boss's wife, the biggest gossip in the hospital, sat at their table. She leaned forward and gazed between the two of them like a tabloid reporter given an exclusive. She smiled a wicked grin that he knew meant trouble. "Dr. DeAngelo, she's beautiful. When are you going to marry this girl?"

Oh God, if only the woman knew the truth.

Chapter Two

Olivia wanted to strangle the older woman. With that simple comment, she'd brought up the past and ruined the mending of their relationship that Olivia had been trying to create with a little trust. Tension flowed from Tony like a beacon searching the river for a dead body, aimed and sharp. Her quick thinking to salvage his speech had left an impression on him, and now that single word, *marry*, had destroyed whatever progress she'd made.

Not that she wanted to pick up where they'd left off, but maybe by healing their wounds, they could both begin again. Because obviously, neither one of them had moved on with someone else. They were both unmarried. Was it because of the past or something more?

She'd tried, lord knows she'd done everything in her power to forget the way Tony made her feel. But no man had even come close to having her searching for him in a crowd or hungering for his touch or loving the way his laugh made her feel.

Tony couldn't be replaced in her heart. Being with him tonight was resurrecting feelings she'd hoped were buried in the deepest underground cavern that even a miner could never rescue. Those feelings were better left where they were and tonight was just another job. Another man needing a woman at his side. Another dollar towards her sibling's college degrees.

"A serious surgeon has no time for a wife," Tony said.

The plagiarized words were a direct quote from his mother and they stung. For a moment, Olivia felt like she'd been bitch slapped. She took a deep breath and reminded herself, this was just a job. A night of looking beautiful on a lonely man's arm.

"Excuse me, my husband is a surgeon," the woman said, her voice outraged. "Oh, honey, a serious surgeon needs a woman to keep his everyday life under control. You guys need keepers. While your brain is working on how to save a patient, your wife is making sure you've got clean clothes, fed, hydrated and rested. We're the glue that keeps the genius working."

Olivia sat stunned by the woman's words. In some ways they made perfect sense. And yet, Tony's mother Mary and father Sergio, had made sure their son would go into his surgical residency with his million dollar brains unattached. He'd gone to New York to become a world-renowned surgeon while she'd stayed home and become the parent to her orphaned siblings.

Alone. Heartbroken. And damn angry, that the man she loved had not even had the decency to come find out what happened. He'd just left town like she was yesterday's news.

"Maybe for some doctors, Mrs. Thornton, but I'm really not marriage material."

"You can say that again," Olivia said.

He gave her a sharp look that reminded her she was to smile and keep her mouth shut.

She turned her attention to Olivia, who felt her neck bristle with warning. "And you're okay with just being his lover?"

Olivia smiled and laid her hand on Tony's arm remembering her job while wanting to scream at both of them for their ignorance. "Tony and I are quite happy in our current situation. There are no expectations for either one of us."

The woman shook her head. "Oh my, you're living together."

"No," Tony said. "She insists on having her own place."

He patted her hand that lingered on his arm, his muscles firm beneath her touch. A tingle spread through her like warm raindrops sliding over wet skin leaving a trail of fire. She swallowed, pushing the feeling down.

"All that intelligence under one roof gets on my nerves."

The woman laughed. "I understand exactly."

God, no, not again. She didn't want to have these feelings for him. She wanted to do her job and go home to her cat and forget all about Dr. Antonio DeAngelo.

He grabbed her hand and brought it to his lips. The feel of his mouth against her flesh had memories rushing at her like a Lamborghini at Monte Carlo. They'd spent their college days exploring each other's bodies like explorers on the hunt for a new continent.

Those had been the best days of her life. And yet she'd walked away from him. Walked away when she needed him most in her life.

They'd dated through college, medical school, and planned to marry when he received orders his residency would be at St John's Hospital in New York City. The premier location to learn cardiology. A dream residency for Tony.

"You two are such a beautiful couple. You should marry her, Dr. DeAngelo. You'd have gorgeous children."

He smiled but didn't respond. The director of the program walked up to the podium. It was almost show time and suddenly Olivia felt nervous for Tony. This was his dream. His confirmation that he'd made the right choices in life so many years ago. And deep inside she felt proud of what he'd accomplished with her not by his side. His parents should be happy.

"Marriage is quite impossible for us," she said.

"It wouldn't work," Tony assured the woman.

Tony was a world-renowned heart surgeon who obviously had no one in his life. Somewhere along the way, he'd become so focused on his career that his personal life was not only in the toilet, but it'd been flushed into the sewer. This big, beautiful, strong man seemed lonely and lost. Sadly, in a room full of people who all knew of him, but not the man personally. Not a single person he'd introduced her to was what she'd consider a close friend. They were all acquaintances. Friendless.

"Actually, we were engaged once," she said.

"Oh really?" the woman said, like she'd just learned a piece of juicy gossip.

He kicked Olivia under the table and she turned to him and smiled knowing that was her warning to shut up. But the devil inside goaded her on. Yes, she'd agreed to look pretty on his arm, but this man needed a wake-up call. Life wasn't just about success.

Dr. Tony's life needed a heart transplant. He needed someone to show him that while his professional life was rocketing to the moon, his personal life sucked sour lemons.

"You're the one that ended the engagement," he responded.

She'd opened this drum full of worms and yet she couldn't seem to stop herself from responding. "You really don't want to go there," she said. "Not now."

"Why? I'm not the one who left you at the altar. You're the one who had me in front of the entire church, waiting on the woman who I thought loved me and wanted to be my wife."

Just then the speaker went to the podium and began to give announcements.

In a whisper loud enough the older woman could hear her, she said, "I wanted to be your wife in the worst possible way. You should ask your mother and father about who ended our engagement."

He turned to look at her just about the time that they called him up on the stage.

For a moment she felt bad as she watched him orient himself, giving her one last frown before he stood and walked to the podium.

Chapter Three

Tony stared out at the audience, looked across the sea of faces and felt his mouth go dry. He glanced down at Olivia and she smiled at him with enough wattage to make his knees weak. Something about her last comment had bells ringing through his head like a five alarm fire.

Three months before they were to marry, her parents had been killed in a tragic car accident, leaving her to care for her younger brother and sister. He'd fully expected to have a ready-made family when he married her, but then she'd left him standing at the altar. Like a coward, she'd run and they hadn't seen each other since. And now here she was back in his life once more.

Rapidly he gave his speech, his mind processing what he needed to say, while the other part of his brain took a look back at all those years ago, when he'd been ready to promise her forever. Like a speeding train, all the anger, hurt and confusion rushed at him, crushing his chest with more emotion than he'd felt in years.

Was this how a heart attack felt? A pulverizing of your organ that left you feeling weak and almost dead? Would he die before he learned the truth from Olivia?

The rational part of his brain gave his diagnosis as anxiety. But his feeling side told him it was pure panic. What happened that day that he didn't understand?

"So in conclusion, I want to thank you for this wonderful honor"

Members of the audience stood and applauded while he walked down from the stage. Thank God this night was almost over. All he had to do was get Olivia out of here and into the limo. They had things to discuss. Life altering decisions were made that day without his input and he needed to understand why she'd chosen to leave him waiting.

He walked to her at their table. "Grab your purse we're leaving."

"But it's not over."

"We're leaving," he said, and helped her from her chair.

She gave a little wave to the woman who was sitting there staring. He placed his hand on the small of her naked back. Her skin was warm to his touch and he felt that sizzle all the way through him straight to his groin. Quickly, he ushered her out the door, wondering just how easy that dress would slide down her body and if she wore underwear beneath that slinky gown.

Suddenly he had to know. He wanted to explore her body one last time. He wanted to return to his youth and learn what had kept her from the church that day.

"Dr. DeAngelo?" Barbara said, running after him as they walked out of the banquet door. "Why are you leaving so soon?"

He turned and smiled at the bewildered woman.

"My medical career has been put on hold while I deal with my personal life," he said, his voice firm as he realized for the first time that his life was empty. There was no one, but his parents and even they were in their late eighties. He was alone.

Olivia was staring at him like she'd seen a monster. And maybe she had.

"I'll take a cab home," she said quietly.

"No, you're not going anywhere. We need to talk. Come back to my hotel room with me," he said. "I need to understand."

She stared at him, her brow furrowing the way a heart contracts only softer. "I don't know if that's a good idea."

"It's private and you owe me an explanation."

She thought for a moment and finally, nodded her head. "Okay, maybe it is time for some explanations."

The limo was waiting for them. When the driver opened the luxury car's door, she slid inside, her dress revealing her long, smooth thighs as tempting as a heart valve replacement. Her brilliant eyes gazed at him with curiosity. God, he wanted her more today than he had when he was nothing more than a broke resident, racking up a truck load of student debt.

"Coming, Tony?" she asked, her long sleek legs bare and naked and so alluring.

He climbed into the car. "Why did you make that comment about my mother?"

"Maybe you should ask her," she said. "How are your parents?"

Oh, he would definitely ask his mother about her comment, but he wanted to hear why Olivia would say such a thing. Yet, right now, it wasn't his mother he was thinking about. Years had passed since he'd experienced great sex. And even then the intercourse had never equaled to what he had with Olivia. His memories of the two of them were hotter than a chili pepper and so much sweeter.

"They've moved into a retirement village where Dad can play golf every day."

She nodded just as the car turned a corner a little too sharp, sending her sliding over to him. He automatically wrapped his arms around her, pulling her body safely up against his. A sultry musk scent enveloped him, the feel of her breasts warm against his shoulder. Desire coursed through his blood at an unhealthy rate and all thoughts of talking ceased.

Tony wanted one thing and only one thing. Olivia.

He gazed into her emerald eyes and experienced his world unraveling. Her arms offered a sense of homecoming as memories of the two of them entangled and naked rocked him.

Red lips beckoned him like a sea nymph luring him to his destruction. Her tongue slid across her lips and he couldn't resist. With a groan, he placed his hands on her head and pulled her mouth to his. He'd loved her more than medicine, more than family, more than any man could ever want a woman and she'd tossed his affections aside. But why?

His mouth roved over hers, melding her lips to his as she opened to his onslaught of passion. Her hands came up and grasped the back of his neck, trailing her fingers along his ears. Gently, he laid her on the seat of the limo, their bodies touching everywhere.

Oh God, he felt like this was where he belonged.

Running his hand beneath her dress, his fingertips skimmed up her smooth leg, until he found the edge of her panties and slipped his fingers beneath the scrap of lace. Like they were back in college, he retraced the familiar steps until he touched her womanly folds.

She broke the kiss and pushed back away from him, her eyes wild, her breathing quick as she stared at him. "We're not talking," she stammered. "We're playing with fire."

He smiled. That had been their code words when things were getting a little too advanced while they were in college. "Be careful or you're going to get burned."

She looked away and when she glanced back at him, there were tears in her eyes. "I already have."

Just then the limo came to a halt. Tony pulled down her dress as he waited for the driver to open the door and then slid out. He helped Olivia alight from the car. He took her hand and pulled her into the entrance to the hotel. Hurriedly, he walked through the lobby to the elevators, his hand holding hers tightly, fearful she would change her mind and runaway. Once on the elevators, he glanced down at Olivia while she stood beside him quiet, contemplative. Her full mouth so tempting, her body trembling.

She turned to say something and he grabbed her head and pulled her lips to his. He didn't want to hear reason, excuses or any logical talk. Not now. Not when he needed her so badly.

He slammed her against the wall of the elevator. At first she resisted and then she relaxed against him, her hands coming up to caress his hair. He pressed his body against hers, his erection nestled against her belly.

He shouldn't want her so badly. He shouldn't crave her like he wanted his next breath. But he did and she was here, his for the taking.

Contract be damned.

She placed her hands between them and pushed just as the bell on the elevator dinged.

"What do you want to talk about?" she said breathlessly as they stepped out of the elevator.

Tony knew exactly what he wanted to talk about, but first he wanted to get them inside. And second, she was his for the evening. His escort. Longing for Olivia had filled him the moment he saw her sitting in that limo waiting for him. Now he was determined to explore her body one last time. Just one last taste before he put her aside forever. Before he moved on for eternity.

He opened the door to his suite and she walked in ahead of him. She turned towards him to say something and he pulled her in his arms. His mouth covered hers again as he walked her to the bed.

She pulled back breaking the seal. "You said we were going to talk.

"We are," he said, and lowered his mouth back to her. He kissed her like a man who had a drought of women for so long that he'd forgotten the feel of lips beneath his. The way a woman softly moaned deep in her throat. The way she made him feel manly and strong.

Ten years had passed since he'd kissed Olivia and yet it felt like he'd never forgotten the way he craved the touch of her mouth. His hand slid down the back of her head, her neck, to her breasts. The low cut of her dress made it easy for him to slip inside and touch her satiny skin. He tweaked her nipple and she groaned, the sound low and deep in her throat.

With ease, he unsnapped the halter top of her dress, exposing her breasts. He leaned down and suckled her nipple into his mouth. She arched her back crying out. "We can't do this. We're supposed to be talking."

"We're speaking with our bodies," he said, his voice deep and husky.

"Oh God," she said, as he moved from one breast to the other. "There's so much we need to say."

"We're saying it right now," he whispered. He reached behind her and found the zipper on her dress. In a matter of moments, he was unzipping her skirt. He stepped back as the silken material fell in a swoosh to the ground. She stood before him naked except for a strip of panties and her heels.

There was no turning back. Breathing was next to impossible as he stared at her firm breasts and narrow waist. All the love he'd felt for her before smacked him in the heart and left his chest aching. Good God, what had he just done?

~

Olivia stood naked in front of the man that she realized she'd never stopped loving. Sure there had been other men in her past, but no one came close to Tony. No one had captured her heart or left her wanting or needing like this man. Tony had a way of making her laugh, disregard her obligations and enjoy life once again.

Though she kept telling him they needed to talk, deep down the only language she wanted to express was with her body. Right now she wanted to feel Tony surging within her. She wanted his fingers to do all the talking in a language only they knew. One where they both rode a rocket to Mars, orbited the moon and returned to earth totally shattered.

She reached for his tuxedo tie and quickly untied the satin strip of fabric and tossed the silk to the floor. Slipping his jacket off, she hurriedly reached for his shirt, undoing the buttons as quickly as her fingers would slip them through the button holes. She slid the shirt off his chest to reveal his smooth skin. God he was more beautiful than she remembered. Her fingertips skimmed over the solid muscles of his chest and abdomen. He let out a hissed rush of breath and she smiled with pleasure.

Even after all these years, he still responded like a man who hungered for her and she quickly undid his belt, unhooked his pants and eased his zipper down. She pushed underwear aside, letting the fabrics pool at his ankles.

His erection sprang at her, hard and rigid and eager. She wrapped her fingers around his strong penis, fisting him as she stroked him. Kneeling on the floor she took him in her mouth, her lips enveloping his hard male member. A groan echoed in the room and she knew she'd pleased him. Like an ice cream cone, she licked him, her tongue running up one side and down the other, stopping to pay special attention to the head.

"Olivia," he moaned.

Tonight would be theirs to last them to eternity. Tonight, she would heal the wound she'd created in his heart and then leave him once more.

He pulled her up. "Enough."

Sinking down onto the bed, he quickly shed his shoes, socks and pants until he was gloriously naked. He pulled her down on the bed with him, skin against skin. Desire flooded through her like a spring thunderstorm.

For a moment, they stared at one another and then his mouth skimmed over hers before his lips went lower. Olivia's mind halted as she let the feelings he was evoking wash over her, reveling in the sensations he created. Tony's scent enveloped her like a tantalizing piece of chocolate, evoking memories she'd long forgotten. Like their bodies had been reawakened to their past and once again were in tune together.

When his tongue swept across her breast, she arched her back in a fevered response. Heat blazed from her breasts to her belly, leaving her wanting and needy. Urgent to touch him, eager to feel him, she reached out and ran her fingertips down his face in a loving caress. They'd always been so good together. Up until that last morning…she pushed the thought out of her head.

Now was not the time for reflecting, only feeling.

Flicking his tongue across her nipple, he moved further down the bed, his mouth trailing kisses. His hands reached for her knees and he spread her legs, opening her up for him.

"Beautiful," he whispered as his tongue delved between her legs.

"Oh," she cried, as she arched her back off the bed gripping the spread as his mouth teased her. This brilliant man humbled himself between her legs, lovingly licking her inner folds, teasing, sending fire spiraling through her.

Unable to stop herself, she gripped the top of his head holding his mouth against her. It had been years since she'd had a man give her an orgasm. Years since anyone had ever put their mouth upon her. Years that she'd given up on finding another man like Tony.

She'd been young, insecure, with more responsibilities than any young woman deserved and yet she'd believed he loved her.

Tension radiated from her center holding her hostage until she gave into the pleasure and screamed Tony's name. The orgasm gripped her and rode her like a rodeo star.

When it was over, she lay there panting, breathing hard. Tony crawled between her legs. Ripping the condom package open he quickly sheathed himself.

"Oh God, Olivia, I can't wait," he said, and plunged deep inside her.

She welcomed him as he slid within the confines of her body, gripping him inside her, holding him tightly with her heart. As if he realized the impact of what they were doing, he paused and then he slowly eased almost all the way out, before plunging in once again. Her need rose rapidly and she opened her eyes and stared deep into his sapphire ones, wanting to touch his soul and brand him as her own. He should have been her husband, he should be her man.

Unhurried, he took her mouth, his lips consuming hers. She wanted him to consume her as desire rippled through her like an aftershock. Their tongues mated and danced as his lips moved over hers. Why with this man did she feel so much passion? Why did her body respond like it had come home?

"Tony," she said needing him like she needed her next breath.

With each thrust, Olivia met him halfway, her hips moving of their own accord, her body completely in tune with his. They moved as one, in unison, in perfect harmony.

Their lips broke apart and she gasped, her lungs needing more air. "Don't stop."

He smiled down at her and pounded into her again and again and again. Unimaginable pleasure spiraled through her, leaving her breathless and dizzy.

Magic filled her, tightening, centering and sizzling with an intensity that only Tony could create. Like an arching bolt of lightning, the feelings from the past and today converged.

With no one else had she ever experienced such pleasure.

His blue eyes darkened as his body shuddered his release. Olivia let go of the orgasm she'd felt gathering like a storm inside her body. Tremors rippled through her. She clasped his back, holding him tightly, wanting to absorb him into her soul, where she could cherish these moments together. There was no getting over this man. He was hers. And though he probably would never have her, there would be no one else for her.

He slumped on top of her and then rolled them to their sides. For a moment the two of them lay there as their breathing returned to normal and their heartbeats slowed.

The room was silent except for the sound of their lungs spasming for more air. Reality crashed in like a two ton rock, making her realize what she'd just done with the man she'd left at the altar.

The intention had been to talk, but once he'd kissed her, there was no going back. No stopping at yellow, red, but a headlong dash to his hotel room. Passion had always been like dynamite between them. Once ignited, there was no turning back.

"I think I should go," she said, the words twisting her heart like a boomerang on steroids.

He rolled over on top of her and began to kiss her again. "No. Not yet."

Chapter Four

The next morning she awoke to an empty bed. She listened to see if he was in the bathroom. Memories of the night before washed over her and she realized that they had never talked. They had spent the night making love, passion consuming them again and again. It was like the years apart had never existed and no days had passed without them being together. It was like they'd picked up right where they had left off.

She listened again and then, wrapping the sheet around, her she tiptoed into the bathroom. He wasn't there. He was gone. His suitcase was gone, his shaving gear, everything. He'd left her just like she'd left him at the altar.

Sadness gripped her stomach and left her reeling. She wanted to cry. She wanted to sit down on the floor and bawl like a baby. He'd gotten his revenge. Only his hurt way more. She'd been given hope only to see it dashed away for good.

It was over. One brief night of going down memory lane. One brief night that had reawakened all the feelings she thought she'd buried and covered up. She'd loved him more than any man she'd ever known. He'd always been her first and really her only love.

She found her panties and her dress and threw on her clothes. This morning she would have to do the walk of shame and sneak out of the hotel, catch a cab to her small apartment.

She opened the door and all but ran away from the painful memories of the man she'd loved most of her life. She would have to let her heart heal once again, but her soul was broken. Maybe forever.

~

Tony hurried back upstairs with coffee cups in hand. He'd checked his bags with the bell captain and ordered a cab to take him to his parents. But first he wanted to talk to Olivia one last time, clear up the past and determine if they had a future. After all, last night had shown they still cared for one another. They'd spent the night getting reacquainted with each other's bodies, now he wanted to know if they had a chance as a couple once again.

He carefully balanced the two cups of coffee he'd bought as he approached the door. When he'd left the room, she'd been sound asleep. And he hadn't wanted to disturb her after he'd kept her awake until after dawn.

Sliding the key in the lock, he quietly opened the door. He stepped into the room and immediately noticed that the bed was empty. Her clothes no longer littered the floor. He stepped to the bathroom and noticed that the room was silent.

With a clench, his chest spasmed and he felt his heart pounding. She was gone. Just like before, she'd slipped away and left him. Just like their wedding day, but this time she'd left him alone and not in front of a church full of people.

A sinking feeling like the death of a patient came over him and then anger surged, gripping him like a giant bird's talons.

Damn her! Damn her for running away once again before they'd had a chance to talk. Before they'd had a chance to settle the past.

Once again she'd run. Once again, she'd left him. But this time, she wasn't going to get away. No, this time there would be no quarter.

~

Tony got out of the taxi cab and stood in front of Olivia's apartment. Damn, she was not going to walk away from him a second time. This time he would be the one to tell her goodbye. Though this morning, he had hoped they could talk about the past and maybe even the future.

He pounded on her door. When she opened the portal, he stared at her. She stood there, her hair wet, her green eyes wide in shock.

"You're not walking away from me a second time without talking."

"What are you talking about?" she asked stunned.

"You always run when it gets tough."

"You're the one who left. When I woke up, I was alone."

"Oh no, you weren't alone. I'd gone down to get us coffee. I wanted to wake you in bed, but when I came back, you were gone."

She grabbed him by the arm and pulled him inside. "Let's stop giving my neighbors a show. Now tell me again why you weren't in the room. Because I checked and your suitcase was gone. I thought…" she stopped and stared at him, her emerald eyes were red-rimmed like she'd been crying.

"You thought I was repaying you for leaving me at the altar."

She stared at him, but didn't respond and he knew she'd believed he'd deliberately left her behind.

"I'd taken my bags down to the bell captain and checked them. I planned to come back and wake you. Then I thought we would talk about the past."

She licked her lips. "And in the meantime, I awoke and discovered you were gone."

They glanced at each other and she sighed. "I'm sorry for leaving."

"I'm sorry, for not at least leaving a note," he said. "We never did have that talk. The one where we discuss what happened all those years ago."

Once again, he saw the wariness in her eyes, yet his body ached with the need for her, his heart rising up in his throat. He wanted her so badly, he could have taken her right here in her apartment. Yet, there was so much between them that needed to be resolved.

"Have a seat, Tony."

He sat down on her couch and for the first time since he'd entered the apartment, he glanced around. There were pictures of her brother and sister hanging on the wall. And then he noticed a picture of the two of them from college.

A happy picture of them laughing together.

Why would she have a picture of the two of them still setting out if she didn't care about him?

He glanced back at her and didn't want to talk. Maybe it was best if they left the past buried. All he wanted to do was lay her down on the couch and make love to her.

They stared at one another, heat smoldering in her gaze.

"Who's going first," she asked.

"You. You left me at the altar, not the other way around. I wanted to marry you. I loved you."

She bristled and he knew he'd said the wrong thing. Though his words were the truth, he didn't want to lose what little trust they'd managed to salvage last night and even this morning.

"That's why you never came back to find out why I hadn't shown up for our wedding?" she responded.

He frowned and suddenly that day had more holes in it than Swiss cheese. "What do you mean?"

"Why didn't you come find me?"

"Mother told me you didn't want to talk to me. That same morning, they had me on a plane to the Caribbean with her and my father. From there I went straight to New York."

A tiny seed of unease began to sprout in his conscious. Why had he trusted anyone else to decide the fate of him and Olivia?

"What did you mother or father tell you about that day? If you remember your mother was the one who didn't want us to marry."

He stared at her, his brows coming together in a frown. Now when he looked back, something about that day seemed off.

"That's twice you've mentioned my mother and my father. Why?"

She took a deep breath and released it slowly. "Your mother and I had several conversations before our wedding date. At the rehearsal dinner, your mother pulled me aside. She told me that I was holding you back. That you would never become a great surgeon if we married. "

He shook his head. "My mother wanted us to wait, but she liked you. She thought that we were a good fit."

She nodded her head in agreement. "You're right. She did, up until the moment that my parents were killed and I took on the responsibility of my brother and sister. But she told me that if I moved with them to New York, that you would never finish your residency. That the demands of a family would be too much."

How had he been so clueless? Because he'd trusted his mother and father.

"Why didn't you tell me?" he asked, feeling betrayed. Was she telling him the truth or was this just another trick? Who was being honest? Olivia or his parents?

"The morning of the wedding your father came to me and brought me a blank check. Whatever amount I wanted, he'd write it out, as long as I didn't marry you." She took a deep breath. "He told me that if you really wanted to marry me, you'd come to me. You never did."

"They told me if you loved me, you would contact me."

"So we were both duped into waiting for the other to appear."

The memory of his father disappearing and his mother being nervous gripped him and he felt nauseated by his next question. "And you took the money."

She bristled and he could see the anger radiating from the tightness in her body.

"I took the check. In fact, I still have it if you'd like to see it," she said. "When times got really bad, I was tempted to cash it, but I couldn't. Our marriage would never have worked. Your parents were so against us marrying and at that time we needed their help and support."

"I want to see the check," he said.

She got up and stalked over to a filing cabinet stuck in an alcove that looked like a small office. She dug around in the back of the cabinet searching. After five minutes, she turned and faced him with a small piece of paper in her hand.

Two steps across the room and she shoved the check into his hand. "I think you should take it and leave."

He gazed at his father's handwriting, his chest breaking at how his family had come between them. Shaking his head, he glanced up into her emerald green-filled eyes. "No, we're not finished."

"Yes, we are," she said with finality and went to the door. She opened it. "Last night was a mistake. I don't belong in your world. Your family would never accept me."

"To hell with my family. This is about us."

He shoved the piece of paper into his pocket, picked up his jacket and walked towards the door. His feet seemed to drag with each step. He didn't want to leave, but he knew he needed some time. Time to find out why his parents would do such a horrible thing on his wedding day.

"We're not done," he said, when he reached the door.

"Yes, we are," she said, her voice cracking. "I should have gotten out of that limo last night. I should never have gone back to the hotel with you."

"I'll be back," he said and walked out the door.

Chapter Five

Tony walked in the house through the garage and directly into the kitchen. His mother who he'd called on his way over looked up from the lunch she was preparing and ran to greet him.

She gave him a hug and a kiss on the cheek.

"Son, I'm so glad you have time to come see your father and I. I know we're coming up next month to visit, but it's so lovely to see you now."

"Hi, Mom. Where's Dad?"

"Oh, he's sitting in front of the TV, getting ready to watch football."

His mother's hair was completely gray and yet she still looked the same to him as the day he'd graduated from medical school. She'd been his biggest supporter. The person who had stood behind him and rooted for him all the way. Even now, all he had to do was pick up the phone and call and she would be there for him.

And yet as much as she loved him, he could see how she would have protected him from marrying Olivia. His father did whatever his mother asked him to do. He would have had no problem going to see Olivia and offering her money.

"I need to talk to both of you," he said, taking his mother and directing her towards where his father would be seated in his favorite chair in front of his favorite game.

They walked into the living area and his father looked up. "Son, come on in. The game is just about to start."

"I need to talk to you both," he said. "Can you shut off the TV, Dad?"

His father frowned, but hit the remote control button that ended the cheerleaders dancing like they were in a disco.

"What's up?" he asked, his brows drawn together.

Tony pulled out the folded check and handed it to his father. He watched as his eyes widened with disbelief. Then he glanced at Tony.

"I was always shocked she never cashed this check."

The air seemed to whoosh from Tony's lungs like a cyclone sucking up everything in its path. So it was all true. For a moment, he just let the pain swirl about him, filling the empty places in his heart. He hadn't wanted to believe Olivia, though all the signs were there. He'd wanted to think that there had been a terrible misunderstanding.

But now he needed to understand.

"Why?"

His mother laid her fingers on his arm. "Now, Tony, you were just starting your residency. You didn't have time for a wife and kids. How could you become the great doctor you are today if you'd had to support her brother and sister. I could have understood you marrying her if she didn't have those children."

He glanced at his mother, anger spiraling like a shooting fountain through him. "What did you want her to do with them? Put them in foster care?"

"Of course not, son, but it was not the right time in your life to take on the responsibility of raising children."

He bit his lip, his jaw twitching with the need to yell at his mother, but he refrained. "Don't you think that was my decision? Don't you think you and Dad took that choice out of my hands?"

His father stood and walked over to him. "Your mother and I did what we thought was best for you. Besides if she'd wanted to marry you, she would not have let a check stop her. She didn't love you enough if she'd take the check."

"Maybe she took the check to make you two look like fools," he said quietly. "I think it worked."

They would always think they'd done what was best for him. They would never see that by interfering they'd hurt him and Olivia in ways that no parents should have the right to do. Yes, Olivia should have come to him, but they hadn't given her the opportunity.

"You stopped her from marrying me. You told her if I wanted to marry her, I'd come to her. And then you got me out of the country before we could find out what you'd done."

"She could have called you, done that texting thing you young people do or whatever to get in touch with you but she didn't," his mother said.

"You're right. She didn't," he said dejectedly. "But now I understand the emergency Caribbean trip."

"It was to help you heal from that botched wedding," his mother said her voice steely, her eyes glaring.

His father looked at the check and then stared at him. "How did you get this check? Did you see her?"

Tony was not about to tell his parents that she'd been his escort to last night's event. He wasn't about to let them know that they'd spent the night together.

"We ran into each other last night."

"Is she married?" his mother asked.

"She's never married," Tony replied.

"Oh dear," she said, a blanched expression on her face. "I guess no other man wanted to raise her parent's children."

"Or maybe she's still in love with me," he said.

They stood there and stared at one another, the atmosphere in the room tense. He clenched his fists, his nails digging into his palm. They were old, they did what they thought was best for him at the time. How could he remain angry? But he wasn't ready to forgive them just yet.

"I've got to go," he said.

"What?" his mother said. "I made you your favorite dinner."

"I can't stay. I've got some things to clear up."

"You're going to that woman," she said, her voice high, her eyes wide. "You still love her."

He laughed. "You're right, Mom. I do. And this time I'm going to marry her."

~

He'd gone to her apartment and even though he'd banged on her door for at least ten minutes, she'd either been gone or refused to open the door to him. Now, he didn't know what to do. He felt lost and as if everything he'd worked so hard for in his life had been a complete waste of time. Sure what he did was important, but what about his personal life? What about a wife and kids and family to carry on his name? What about someone cradling him in the darkness and easing his pain when he'd lost a patient?

Didn't he deserve happiness? Didn't Olivia deserve happiness?

He'd walked Olivia's neighborhood aimlessly, not certain of where he was going, only feeling the need to move. To exercise the demons plaguing him.

When he looked up, he realized he was in a park. The very park where they had gone together during college. Wistfulness filled him and he longed for that simpler time, before their wedding, when they had been so in love.

He ambled over to their bench and there she sat, gazing at the waterfall, tears running down her face.

"Come here often," he asked.

She glanced up at him, her emerald eyes, sparkling like rhinestones. "I haven't been here since the last time I was with you."

He smiled. Warmth and satisfaction filled all the aching holes in his soul. He was glad she'd never returned to their park. "That's been a few years."

"Yeah, it has."

"Care if I sit down?"

"No, go ahead," she said, moving over to make room for him.

"I spoke to my parents," he said his voice heavy. "I'm sorry."

"It's not your fault," she said. "I should have found you. I should have talked to you about what they were saying, but you were so stressed about the residency. I didn't want to bother you with the details."

Tony hung his head. "I should have talked to you as well."

"Maybe they were right. Maybe we weren't supposed to be together."

He turned her to face him. "No. I don't believe that. Why didn't you tell me?"

"I didn't want my situation to stop you from being a doctor. I wanted you to become the surgeon you'd always dreamed of."

Oh, he'd become the surgeon he wanted to become, but somehow his career felt empty. His life felt incomplete. And there was, Olivia. Until this weekend, he'd never understood exactly what. But now he knew. He'd missed her smile, her infectious nature, the way they'd shared everything. The love that had grown between them. He'd missed her smart-ass nature and the way she was the only woman to ever stand up to him.

He needed someone who knew he put on his underwear just like all other men. Someone who would be honest and truthful with him and love him in spite of his faults. Someone like Olivia. No, not *like* Olivia. He needed his Olivia, his soulmate.

Grabbing her, he put all his emotions into his kiss. He'd loved this woman for a lifetime and he wanted to show her how much she meant to him. He kissed her like a man dying and she was his lifeline. He kissed her like she was his lover. He poured his emotions into his lips and tried to show her how much he wanted her.

She relaxed against him, succumbing to his kiss. She wrapped her arms around him, her body leaning into him.

Coming to Dallas, he'd planned on flying in for the event last night and then right back to New York. Now he wasn't so certain. Now he didn't want to leave.

She pulled back. "Don't you have a plane to catch?"

He did. The flight left in one hour.

His lips covered hers once again. He didn't want to think about his obligations. He didn't want to hurry back to New York. His life had been here until his mother convinced him to go ahead with his residency. After the wedding, he'd listened to his mother's rational reasons why he should go to New York, even when his heart wanted to stay. But he'd followed his dreams and become a surgeon. Now he wondered if he shouldn't have stuck around and helped Olivia. What had she endured these last ten years?

His palms came up and cradled her face while his lips continued to explore the deep recesses of her mouth. He'd loved her heart and soul. After her parents died, he'd cradled her in his arms and promised her he'd never leave her, but yet at the first sign of trouble, he'd run. Sure she'd left him at the altar, but how could his mother and father have convinced her that he didn't need her in his life at that time?

Sliding his hands down her face, he pressed his body against hers, the need rising up in him once again. With Olivia in his arms, he felt as if he'd come home. Like the missing part of him had been filled.

Their lips came apart. "I'll walk you home."

The three short blocks were a tension-filled silence. Once they reached her apartment, he followed her in. He was going to miss his flight and he didn't care. He didn't care that he'd not arrive back to New York until late. For the first time in ten years, he'd miss a day of work and he didn't care. He cared about Olivia.

She turned towards him and his hands reached for her. He needed her filling him like the blood that churned his life force within him. Their lips came together, an infusion of long lost love and dreams from their youth.

As he kissed her, he walked her backwards, to her bedroom. She didn't fight him or tell him no as he slowly removed her shirt. Her fingers began to unbutton his dress shirt. Their lips parted and they stared at each other, their breathing heavy and soon the two of them were tearing at each other's clothing.

Heat radiated from him as he removed her blouse, her bra, her pants. When they both were naked, he took her hand and they fell onto the bed.

"God, you're so beautiful," he whispered as his hand slowly traveled from her face to her breasts. He slid his naked body against hers. "I can't wait to be inside you."

"Tony," she gasped as she wrapped her fingers around his hardened shaft. He'd been hard since he walked in the door. Filled with lust and longing for her.

His mouth covered hers and he traced the edge of her lips with his tongue, craving her like a man dying of thirst in the desert. He suckled her mouth, needing her to fill him with her sweetness. She returned his kiss, shocking him at the hunger radiating from her. Hunger for him and that left him crazy with desire for her.

Her skin felt like silk as he held her face, refusing to let her go. They kissed for minutes, expressing with their bodies what they could not say with words.

Reaching between them, his fingers stroked her breast, her skin soft as she moaned deep within her throat.

"Touch me," he pleaded, needing to feel her caress. She ran her fingertips across his chest, her stroke leaving trails of fire.

The heat of her gaze made him ache with need. A need that had been denied for too many years.

Tony bent over her breast, closing his mouth around her nipple. She clenched her fists in his hair as he lovingly kissed each breast. Between her legs, his hand touched her moist tender folds and she cried out, "Tony."

"I'm here, baby," he said, his mouth around her nipple as he sucked the tender orb.

He wanted more. He wanted her surrounding him as he plunged deep inside her body. He positioned himself over her, his knee gently spreading her legs. This was where he belonged, here with her, loving her every day, sharing her joys, her pains, her life.

His lips covered her mouth as gently he eased inside her, feeling her body spreading to accommodate him. The human body was a miraculous thing he'd loved since he was a young boy. And sex with Olivia felt like he'd come home to where he belonged.

Moving within her, he felt the tension rise up in him even stronger. He plunged into her body as she took him to even greater heights. Nails raking down his back, her moans grew louder, her breathing harsh.

Sure he'd had other women, but none of them had ever pleasured him or made him feel like a man, the way Olivia did. She was the woman who'd held his heart in her hands since he'd been a med student. She was the woman who'd understood and accepted his need to succeed and had helped him study to reach his dreams. She was the woman who even today had his pulse racing and his heart spinning out of control.

He needed her in his life.

Tony wanted to suspend time and remain here locked in the depths of her body, giving and receiving pleasure, but knew in just a matter of time he'd lose all control. He couldn't last long with her gripping him deep inside as he pushed deep within her.

Only with Olivia had he ever felt loved. This was the reason he'd never found anyone else. She was his true love.

He wanted to hold back, but knew he couldn't. Just then she started to spasm out of control, her body gripping him tightly and he joined her headlong over the cliff as his world spiraled out of control.

Collapsing on top of her, he rolled them to their sides while his breathing slowed and his heart rate came back to a normal rhythm.

For several minutes they laid there and he enjoyed the rightness of the moment. It felt so good to be holding her in his arms, lying in bed together.

"You need to go," she said softly. "You're going to miss your flight."

"Already have," he replied. "We were good together."

"Yes, but that doesn't mean it would be the same now."

"No, but I think last night and today shows us that we're still very attracted to each other." If not in love, he wanted to add, but feared she would bolt at the words.

She nodded . "We're very good together. But your life is not what it should be. You're married to your career. You have very few friends and no one important in your life. I want more."

Her words were true. He was dedicated to his career and friends had always seemed more of a hassle than a necessity.

"What do you want, Olivia?" he asked.

"I want to be married and to someday have children."

"I want the same things," he said, realizing it was true. He wanted a family of his own, someone to come home to who loved and understood him. Olivia accepted and appreciated him.

"I want to have meaningful connections with people. I want my children to know their father."

Pain seared through him stinging is bruised emotions at the thought that she didn't realize that the two of them would be more important than anything else in this world. Anything.

"You and our children would be the most important thing in my life." He frowned. "As for everyone else, I try. I really do, but people are intimidated by me. They don't want me to be their friend. Just their colleague."

Wasn't this his biggest problem now? He was a loner, someone who had never had an easy time making friends.

"Even in college, you had no meaningful friends. And last night…you didn't have anyone there that cared about you."

"I agree. Only you and that wasn't on purpose. But I don't know how to change that." And he wasn't certain he wanted to. Maybe that was where a wife could make a difference in his life.

She stared at him and shook her head. "If you can't have a meaningful relationship with a friend, how do you know it would work with us?"

The reason he knew was because he would make it work. The woman had wrapped herself around his heart years ago and even a botched wedding had not released him from her spell.

"I just do. I need you in my life. Last night showed me that we were meant for each other. That there is still love between us."

She nodded. "Maybe. But being with people I love and cherish and care about is more important than my career.

You've got to prove to me that you feel the same way. You need to show me that you care more about our relationship than you do about your career."

"I can't give up medicine," he said knowing in his heart that would be his kryptonite.

"I'm not asking you to. I'm asking you to show me that you can have a relationship where I'm more important and any children we may have would come before your career."

He frowned. How could he prove that to her? He believed her request was possible, but how could he show her she would be the most important person in his life? "You're asking the impossible. I can't give up medicine for anyone."

"And you don't understand. So I don't think this is going to work."

Olivia rose from the bed and went into the bathroom. When she returned, she had a robe on. "I think you should go."

He gazed up at her, his heart breaking inside his chest, his mind screaming, no, not again. Never again. What had he done wrong? Why wouldn't she give them a chance?

"It was great to see you again and I want to wish you the best of luck with everything."

He slowly rose from the bed and dressed, clearly not happy that she was basically giving him the brush off, or at least that's what it seemed. Anger surged through him and he wanted to prove to her that she couldn't give up.

Tony knew one thing he could do. He grabbed her and put all his emotions into his kiss. He'd loved this woman for a lifetime and he wanted to show her how much she meant to him. you've used these phrases before He kissed her like a man dying and she was his lifeline. He poured his emotions into his mouth and tried to show her how much he wanted her.

When he released her, she had tears swimming in her eyes. "Please, just go."

"What would it take for me to prove to you that if we were married you would be the most important person in my life? Tell me, so that I know how to demonstrate what you need."

She blinked the tears from her eyes, her face confused and surprised. "How many hours a week do you work?"

He shrugged. "Almost eighty."

She shook her head. "You could change those hours, but even then, what's to keep you from going back to your eighty hour work week once we're married?"

For years, his colleagues had been telling him he was on the path to burnout and he knew they were right, but there had been no one to go home to. There had been nothing in his life but medicine.

He grabbed her by the arms and pulled her in close. "I'm making a vow to you right now, that I will change to working only fifty hours a week for the rest of my life if you'll marry me. I'll make friends, I'll get involved with some social kind of nonsense if you'll commit to being my wife."

"It's not going to work," she said.

"Now who's not willing to make a commitment," he said. "I'm willing to change my life for you, but you're still saying no. I think you're the one who's afraid."

"You're right, I am afraid. I don't think you can do it. And I don't want to be hurt yet again."

There was nothing he enjoyed more in life than a good challenge. The challenge to save a patient's life, to graduate medical school, to show Olivia once and for all that she was all that mattered. He could do this.

He released her. "My assistant is the most honest woman I know. She won't lie for anyone. For the next two months, she will keep track of my hours. I will also have

her verify that I'm involved with some social activity.
You'll be hearing from her and from me. At the end of two
months, if you don't agree to be my wife, then you'll never
hear from me again."

"You can't do it," she said softly. "It's just not in your
nature."

He reached for her and kissed her soundly, his lips
promising that nothing in his life was more important than
proving his career would take second place to her.

When he finished kissing her, he stepped back. "You'll
be hearing from me every day and Raylene, my assistant,
will be sending you updates. In two months, I'll be back in
Dallas and at that time you can give me your decision
about marriage. And don't expect a long engagement."

She smiled. "Two months. Tony, if you find you can't
do this, all you have to do is call and tell me."

"Oh, I'm going to call you all right, but it's going to be
to talk to you." He ran his fingers along her face.
"Goodbye, Olivia. See you in two months."

Chapter Six

Two months later, excitement filled Olivia and as she thought how her life had changed since fate had intervened and returned Tony to her. When she'd said goodbye to him that long sixty days ago, she'd known that no matter what, she would marry him. But not as the overworked doctor who put medicine before everything. Sure he was a great cardiac surgeon, but even great men deserved a pleasant life.

If he'd failed at the tasks she set out for him, she would have accepted him, but this way he'd changed and grown and now she couldn't wait to become his wife. And he'd insisted she quit the escort service and had given Caitlyn a ten thousand dollar donation to finish her degree.

Helping her sister had just made her love him even more.

He'd told her he would be here at five and it was five ten. She was starting to get worried.

A knock sounded. She ran to the door and flung it open. There he stood with flowers in his hand and a bottle of champagne.

She threw her arms around him. "It's so good to see you."

"Sorry, I'm late, but you know Dallas traffic has gotten worse since the time I left."

"Yes, it has. Come in."

They'd talked on the phone every day, sometimes two and three times a day. He'd fulfilled every task she'd given him and now played golf once a week with several other doctors from the hospital. He also ended his day at five unless he had an emergency surgery and then he took Friday off.

He'd given his staff Friday off as well and saw patients four days a week. Once he'd worked over the fifty hours and it had been to save the life of a twelve year old boy. How could she fault him for that and the next week, he'd made up the difference and worked forty hours. The man seriously was trying to meet her every demand. And she loved him more each day.

He sat down on the couch and an awkward silence fell between them. He handed her the flowers. "These are for you."

She smiled. "I kind of thought so, but wanted you to give them to me first."

He laughed. "God, I feel like I'm seventeen years old again."

She hurriedly put the flowers away and then came back to sit beside him on the couch. "How are you?"

"I'm so good. I just want to pick you up and carry you into the bedroom and ravish you all night long."

Olivia felt her heart pounding in her chest at the thrill of being together again. "That sounds really nice."

"But we can't."

Her insides went cold. "Why not?"

"I've done everything you've asked and frankly, I think it's made me a better doctor. I'm no longer on the road to burnout. I enjoy my job so much more than ever before. There's only one thing missing in my life now. I need you."

She smiled. He had no idea how much she needed him. But she'd wait until he was finished before she told him.

"I love you. I want to wake up beside you each morning. I want to come home to you at night. I want to share your joys, your trials, your smiles and your laughter. I want you beside me when I take my last breath. Marry me, Olivia. Marry me and make me a better man."

Joy consumed her pushing out the past and eager for the future. She threw back her head and laughed. "You don't know how good that makes me feel."

"Then say yes and fly away with me tonight to Vegas. We'll get married this weekend, just the two of us and spend the rest of our lives together. The limo is waiting for us outside and I have two tickets for us to leave tonight."

Getting married in Vegas sounded wonderful. There would be no one to stop them. And the idea of being with him all weekend left her giddy with excitement.

She threw her arms around him. "There's one problem left for us to resolve."

"What? Tell me."

She swallowed feeling nervous for the first time today.

"I can't drink champagne. Is that okay?"

He leaned back and frowned at her like she was crazy. "I don't care. I just want to marry you. I love you Olivia."

"I love you so much, Tony. I always have. And you're going to have an instant family."

"I should have had an instant family ten years ago, when were supposed to marry," he said with force.

Suddenly his face changed and his eyes widened. "Oh my God. You're pregnant."

She smiled. "We forgot to use protection that last time we made love. We're going to have a baby."

He grabbed her and wrapped his arms around her. "Somehow the past has repeated for us, but this time, I'm not letting you out of my sight until we're married."

"And this time, no one can stop me from marrying you. I love you so much, Tony. I always have."

Tony's lips covered hers. When they finally came up for air, he gazed at her with such love that she could feel the emotion radiating from him. "I can't wait to begin our life together."

He jumped up from the couch and grabbed her by the hand. "Come on, let's go get married in Vegas."

She laughed. "But I don't have a bag packed."

"You don't need one. You're going to be naked in my bed."

A frown appeared on his face and he pulled her to him. "Promise me you won't ever leave me."

She smiled and brushed back a lock of his hair. "I promise you, Tony that I will never leave you. You have me until death parts us."

"Right back at you, baby." He kissed her and then pulled her towards the door. "Look out Vegas, here we come."

Thank you for reading!

Dear Reader,

Thank you for purchasing *Paying for the Past*, my short sexy novella. I know that your choices of authors and books are limitless. I'm flattered that you chose my book and hope you enjoy reunion stories as much as I do. There will be additional books in the Racy Reunion series, so continue to check back often.

If you'd like to learn when I publish new books, please sign up for my Newsletter. Again, I appreciate your interest and I hope you enjoy Tony and Olivia's story.

Yours in Drama, Divas, Bad Boys, and Romance!
Sincerely,
Sylvia McDaniel

Books by Sylvia McDaniel

Contemporary Romance

Standalones
The Reluctant Santa
My Sister's Boyfriend
The Wanted Bride
The Relationship Coach
Her Christmas Lie
Secrets, Lies, and Online Dating
Paying for the Past
Cupid's Revenge

Anthologies
Kisses, Laughter & Love
Christmas with you

Collaborative Series

Magic, New Mexico
Touch of Decadence

Western Historicals

Standalones
A Hero's Heart
A Scarlet Bride
Second Chance Cowboy

The Cuvier Women
Wronged
Betrayed
Beguiled

Lipstick and Lead
Desperate
Deadly
Dangerous
Daring
Determined
Deceived

Scandalous Suffragettes
Abigail
Bella
Callie
Faith

The Burnett Brides
The Rancher Takes a Bride
The Outlaw Takes a Bride
The Marshal Takes a Bride
The Christmas Bride

Anthologies
Wild Western Women
Courting the West
Wild Western Women Ride Again

Collaborative Series

The Surprise Brides
Ethan

American Mail Order Brides
Katie

About the Author

Sylvia McDaniel is a best-selling, award-winning author of historical romance and contemporary romance novels. Known for her sweet, funny, family-oriented romances, Sylvia is the author of The Burnett Brides, a western historical western series, The Cuvier Widows, a Louisiana historical series, and several short contemporary romances.

She is the former President of the Dallas Area Romance Authors, a member of the Romance Writers of America®, and a member of Novelists Inc. Her novel, A Hero's Heart, was a 1996 Golden Heart Finalist. Several other books have placed or won in the San Antonio Romance Authors Contest and the LERA Contest, and she was a Golden Network Finalist.

Married for nearly twenty years to her best friend, they have two dachshunds that are beyond spoiled and a good-looking, grown son who thinks there's no place like home. She loves gardening, shopping, knitting, and football (Cowboys and Bronco's fan), but not necessarily in that order.

Look for her the first Tuesday of every month at the Plotting Princesses blogspot, and be sure to sign up for her newsletter to learn about new releases and contests. Every month a new subscriber is entered into a drawing for a free book!

She can be found online at: www.sylviamcdaniel.com or on Facebook. You can write to Sylvia at P.O. Box 2542, Coppell, TX 750

Looking for a new book to read?

Tyler Ferguson thought losing your memory had some advantages, but mainly it created problems. When a roadside bomb in Kabul exploded the Humvee he'd been riding in, and wiped his memory of the last nine months in Afghanistan, he'd been given a medical leave to come home just in time for Christmas. And Tyler is so excited to see his fiancée, Kelsey Johnson.

Kelsey can't believe it when she opens the door and there stands the man she still loves, but had broken off their engagement while he was deployed. Doubts of being able to live with Tyler in constant danger, of only seeing him several months a year had her ending the relationship.

When she realizes he doesn't remember the breakup, she thinks that life has given her a second chance with the man she loves. At least until his memory returns.

Can a wedding and Christmas heal Tyler and give Kelsey the strength she needs to be a military wife? Can a soldier forgive the girl he loves when she sends him a Dear John letter?

Sneak Peek into Her Christmas Lie

Losing his memory had some advantages, but mainly it created problems. Like how could he forget where Kelsey Johnson, his fiancée, lived? Of course, she'd moved here during the months he liked to call the dark days. He couldn't remember a thing from March to November because a roadside bomb in Kabul had obliterated his Humvee, giving him a near death experience and a one month hospital stay in Germany. All courtesy of Afghan insurgents.

Marine Second Lieutenant Tyler Ferguson shifted restlessly in the back seat of the cab. How would Kelsey react when she saw the bandage on his head and the wound in his leg, which was better, but far from healed? He'd been lucky. His driver, Sargent George McDonald didn't fare as well and he hated that. They'd become friends as he drove him around the desert rebuilding the infrastructure so his fellow marines could communicate and do recon work.

He'd been gone nine months, and for the last two, he'd had no communication with Kelsey. She must be worried sick. Him showing up unannounced, he hoped was a great surprise. He couldn't wait to gaze into her green eyes and let his fingers comb through her silken red curls.

Would it be rude, just to pick her up and carry her straight into the bedroom? He'd missed her so much, his heart ached as the miles separating them shrunk. It'd been so long since he'd felt her warm, loving arms around him.

Just the thought of seeing her, brought tears to his eyes. For a while he'd thought he'd never see her again. But finally his body had responded to the doctors' treatments and then they'd delivered the bad news.

Maybe he'd lost more than just days in a hospital. Maybe he'd lost months, possibly forever, but his mind was working, his body was healing and even his leg was better. He had a lot to be thankful for.

So he couldn't remember the last nine months. The blast seemed to sear away the time he'd been in Afghanistan and frankly, he was okay with that as long as he could remember today and yesterday and every day going forward. Especially if it was spent with the woman he loved.

Snow fell softly as they drove through the Denver, Colorado neighborhood. He'd found her address on Google and given it to the driver. The cab pulled to a stop and he gingerly stepped out, hoping his bad leg held. Paying the driver, he said, "Thanks, man."

"Good luck, soldier," the cab driver said.

Tyler felt a grin spread across his face. Yanking off his cap, he pulled out the Santa hat he'd bought in the airport. With flowers in one hand, his duffle bag in the other, he limped up the sidewalk to the front door.

The home looked inviting, a wide wooden porch, with patio chairs beneath the overhang eves. The neighborhood was an older, more settled type of homeowner. The kind of place with families and dogs and backyard barbecues. The only problem was Kelsey hadn't decorated for Christmas which surprised him. She loved the holiday season and always decked the house from the inside out.

With trembling fingers, he rang the bell and waited impatiently. Just when he was ready to give up, he heard the door locks being pulled back. Anticipation at seeing the woman he loved, tore at his rapidly beating heart. This point in time seemed to drag clear into next week. When she pulled back the wooden door, he opened his arms wide. "Merry Christmas!"

For a moment, Kelsey stared at him in shock and then she came outside. Gently, she reached up and put her hand to his head. He'd waited so long for her loving touch...a whole four weeks, but he knew it'd been longer. "You're hurt."

"Yeah, I had a little meeting with a roadside bomb. But the insurgents didn't live to tell about the destruction they'd caused." The doctors had refused to let him remove the bandage around his head until after the next appointment.

"Tyler," she whispered her voice choked.

Why wasn't she kissing him? Sure, he probably looked worse than he felt, but since the day of the bombing, he'd dreamed about her lips moving against his.

"Are you badly injured?" she asked.

"A little memory loss." He laughed and shrugged, wanting only to kiss her. "I've been anticipating your mouth and all you want to talk about is how badly hurt I am?"

Sweeping her into his arms, he pulled her body in close to him. His lips came crashing down on hers in a kiss that he'd been waiting for. A kiss filled with promises of love and devotion and assurances of nights of mind-blowing sex. He craved some between the sheets action with his woman in a major way.

Her arms slowly wound around him, as she gave herself over to the demands of his mouth. He wanted her as close as he could get her without doing the tango right here on her porch, under the stars, while the neighbors watched.

She stepped out of his arms and stared at him, her emerald eyes shimmering with tears. "Come in, Tyler, we need to talk."